FANTASY
FIELD TRIPS

Adventure to the

PIONEER PRAIRIE!

by Carole Marsh

Managing Editor: Sherry Moss
Senior Editor: Janice Baker
Assistant Editor: Mike Kelly
Cover Design: Vicki DeJoy
Cover and Inside Illustrations: Kirin Knapp (casuallygreen.com)
Content Design: Darryl Lilly, Outreach Graphics

Gallopade International is introducing SAT words that kids need to know
in each new book that we publish. The SAT words are bold in the story.
Look for this special logo beside each word in the glossary. Happy Learning!

Gallopade is proud to be a member and supporter of these educational
organizations and associations:

American Booksellers Association

American Library Association

International Reading Association

National Association for Gifted Children

The National School Supply and Equipment Association

The National Council for the Social Studies

Museum Store Association

Association of Partners for Public Lands

20 YEARS AGO...

As a mother and an author, one of the fondest periods of my life was when I decided to write mystery books for children. At this time (1979) kids were pretty much glued to the TV, something parents and teachers complained about the way they do about web surfing and blogging today.

I decided to set each mystery in a real place—a place kids could go and visit for themselves after reading the book. And I also used real children as characters. Usually a couple of myown children served as characters, and I had no trouble recruiting kids from the book's location to also be characters.

Also, I wanted all the kids—boys and girls of all ages—to participate in solving the mystery. And, I wanted kids to learn something as they read. Something about the history of the location. And I wanted the stories to be funny. That formula
of real+scary+smart+fun served me well.

I love getting letters from teachers and parents who say they read the book with their class or child, then visited the historic site and saw all the places in the mystery for themselves. What's so great about that? What's great is that you and your children have an experience that bonds you together forever. Something you shared. Something you both cared about at the time. Something that crossed all age levels—a good story, a good scare, a good laugh!

20 years later,

Carole Marsh

Hey, kids! As you see—here we are ready to embark on another of our exciting Carole Marsh Mystery adventures! You know, in "real life," I keep very close tabs on Christina, Grant, and their friends when we travel. However, in the mystery books, they always seem to slip away from Papa and I so that they can try to solve the mystery on their own!

I hope you will go to www.carolemarshmysteries.com and apply to be a character in a future mystery book!

Well, The Mystery Girl is all tuned up and ready for "take-off!" Gotta go... Papa says so! Wonder what I've forgotten this time?

Happy "Armchair Travel" Reading,

Mimi

ABOUT THE CHARACTERS

**Ms. Bogus' Fourth Grade
Alpine McAlpine School**

Can you imagine a class where you go on field trips that are literally "out of this world?" The kids in Ms. Bogus' fourth grade class don't just imagine Fantasy Field Trips–they experience them!

Meet Ms. Bogus, the quirky teacher with the big heart and even bigger imagination! On the left are twins Skylar and Drew, and Colette, who sits in a wheelchair but stands tall in the middle of every Fantasy Field Trip adventure! On the right are Lucia, the girl who loves to travel; Willy, the class clown with lots of big ideas; and Sarah, the shy blonde who loves to read.

There are lots of other kids to meet in Ms. Bogus' class, too. So, let's go–it's time for a Fantasy Field Trip!

TABLE OF CONTENTS

Prologue
1 Yella-Bellied Chickin 1
2 Yur Mine, Willy! 5
3 Field Of Battle 11
4 Contagious! 17
5 The Jolly Schooner 21
6 Indian Attack 29
7 Johnnycakes and Butter! 35
8 Cock-a-doodle-doo 41
9 River Ride 45
10 Over the Edge 51
11 Have You Ever Heard of a UFO? 57
12 Home Sweet Home 63
13 This is a Working Farm, Boys! 67
14 Dirt Surfing 73
15 A Saw is a Man's Best Friend 79
16 Family Ties 83
17 Bad Guys! 87
18 Time to Go 95
Epilogue 99
    About the Author 103
    Book Club: Talk About It! 104
    Book Club: Bring it to Life! 106
    Prairie Trivia 107
    Glossary 110
    Pop Quiz 112
    Scavenger Hunt 113
    Tech Connects 114

PROLOGUE

"I'm not sure about this Wild West ranch Ms. Bogus is taking us to," Colette said, her fiery red hair sparkling in the morning sunlight. "I have enough trouble getting around our town in my wheelchair, let alone a town with no sidewalks."

"No sidewalks means no curbs to go up," Skylar suggested. "Maybe that'll make it easier than you think."

Willy leaned his tall frame to the left, as the bus made a right turn on its way to the Living History Farm in Urbandale, Iowa. "We're not going to a Wild West ranch," Willy remarked, as he pulled his

Chicago Cubs cap down over his curly hair. "It's an 1875 prairie town. And all the people that work there actually live like they did back in the late 1800s."

"I 'Googled' it on the Internet," Sarah said, pulling her head up from a book on meteors she was reading. "It sounds pretty cool and they've made everything easy for handicapped people, although Drew may have to continue his job of pushing you up some of the steeper ramps."

Colette twisted around in her chair to see the twins behind her. She had to look at their eyes to be sure which one was Drew and which one was his brother Skylar. They both had shaggy blond hair and were identical in every other way except for their eye color. Drew had striking, cobalt-blue eyes, and Skylar had puppy-dog, chocolate-brown eyes.

"My lord," Colette said, in her best medieval voice, "are you available for hire?"

"Of course, my lady," Drew said, "for a small pittance."

"A pittance?" Colette asked. "I'm afraid, my lord, I have nothing of value."

"Ah, ha, my lady!" Drew said, "but you do. All I require is a ride in your chair, uh, chariot, down a really steep ramp if we can find one."

"My lord," Colette continued, "my chariot is but a small price to pay for your allegiance. Please, just don't break it—or your arms!"

"All right," Willy said. "Stop that! Don't you guys get enough of Shakespeare in Miss Spencer's class?"

"What's wrong, Willy?" Colette asked. "Don't you like Shakespeare?"

"No!" Willy said. "It's just a bunch of gibberish. Besides, we're going to a late

1800s American town, not a late 1500s English town. Ya gotta talk like ya ben plowin' dim der fields, ya buncha tobacca chompin' sodbustin' sidewinders."

"Yeah!" Lucia cried, jumping up, throwing her leg under her, and sitting back down on it. Her curly brown hair bounced back into place. "Ya'll need ta learn ta speak American, not dat English," she added. "Because ya'll are on da prairie now!"

"Oh, boy!" Sarah said, shaking her blond hair back and forth. "I don't know how much of this I can take. Can we go back to Mars, instead?"

CHAPTER ONE:

YELLA-BELLIED CHICKIN!

Sarah stood by the pickle barrel in the general store in the 1875 town of Walnut Hill at the Living History Farm. The store was an exact replica of old-time general stores, which were "one-stop" shops for the local folks. Farmers and townspeople could buy items like hardware, bulk foods, and clothing at one convenient location.

Sarah kept staring at the pickle barrel, trying to decide if she wanted to buy

a pickle or not. She loved pickles. She turned to ask Lucia her opinion.

"Lucia..." She wasn't there. Just a minute ago, Lucia had been standing by the potbelly stove, watching Drew and Willy play checkers on the store's checkerboard. "Hmm!" Sarah remarked. "What kind of trouble are they getting into now?"

Willy peeked around the corner of Mrs. Elliott's Millinery, a store where women back in 1875 would have purchased hats and fashion accessories like parasols, stockings, or jewelry.

He pulled back when he saw Skylar behind a wagon parked in front of the town's Newspaper and Print Shop. He sprinted toward the wagon just as Skylar popped out from behind it.

SPLASH!

Willy's water balloon splattered into Skylar's chest, drenching him. "You're out!" Willy shouted. As he ran past Skylar, he grabbed the water balloon in Skylar's hand and leaped into a hiding place next to the print shop.

Colette was looking for a target when she saw Willy run around the side of the print shop. She was hiding on the other side. "You're mine, Willy!" she said to herself, spinning her chair around to sneak up on him.

SPLAT!

A big orange balloon burst on the top of Colette's shoulder, soaking her hair. "You're out, Colette!" Lucia shouted.

As Lucia grabbed Colette's water balloon from her lap, she heard footsteps on the wooden walkway to her left. It was Drew!

Drew reeled back to throw his balloon, but just as he let go, Lucia dove out of the way. The balloon landed softly in a basket of newspaper.

SPLAT!

Lucia's balloon exploded just above Drew's belt, soaking the front of his pants. She leaped to her feet and scooped the water balloon out of the basket.

She sauntered out into the middle of the street.

"Willy!" Lucia yelled. "Ya yella-bellied chicken. Come out and face me like a man."

CHAPTER TWO:

YUR MINE, WILLY!

Willy ambled out to the center of the street, twenty paces from Lucia. Drew, Colette, and Skylar stood by the print shop to watch the shootout. Ms. Bogus came out of the millinery, just as Sarah emerged from the general store, trailed by a group of other kids in the class.

"You've made fun of my brother fer da last time," Lucia said, tilting her cowboy hat back on her head.

"Yeah!" Willy shouted, pulling his Cubs cap low over his eyes. "And I'm gonna continue ta make fun of him."

"You're mine, Willy!" Lucia said. She moved her arms away from her body, and stared Willy straight in the eyes. "It's your move, pardner."

Willy took a blade of grass out of his mouth, threw it to the ground, and stomped on it. "Ladies first," he said.

Lucia was just about to throw her balloon when she saw Willy's hand move. That threw her timing off and she flung her balloon wildly.

Willy's bluff worked. Lucia had thrown the balloon before she was ready, and it exploded harmlessly behind him.

Willy launched his balloon at Lucia, catching her left shoulder. It burst on impact, soaking her shirt.

The boys in the class cheered for Willy, as he ambled up to Lucia. "You okay?" he asked.

"Yes, I'm fine," Lucia said, "but you cheated."

"Not really," Willy replied. "It's called bluffing and you fell for it. Besides, you know what they say, all's fair in love and war."

The class surrounded the combatants. "You're right," Lucia said, smiling. "That was just a battle. The war's not over yet!" The girls around her burst into **boisterous** applause.

CHAPTER THREE

FIELD OF BATTLE

The Alpine McAlpine fourth grade class fit comfortably into Walnut Hill's one-room schoolhouse, where Ms. Bogus stood at the front of the class.

She was a tall, pear-shaped woman who was completely comfortable in her oversized dress, string of pearls, outdated slip-on shoes, and unbrushed haircut.

She peered over the cat-eye glasses that were always perched on the end of her pointy nose. "This building, class," Ms. Bogus said, "is similar to the one-room schoolhouses of 100 years ago.

"The teacher was usually a young woman in her late teens or early twenties," she continued. "She would teach for a few years before she got married. Many times she was only a few years older than the oldest boys in her class."

"What kind of subjects did she teach?" Sarah asked.

"Mostly math, reading, and writing," Ms. Bogus replied. "School was basically the same back then, except that children were not separated into grades. Students advanced at their own pace. Girls were usually ahead of the boys in their studies," she added.

"So," Lucia said, smiling, "nothing's really changed since then, huh!"

"I wouldn't say that," Ms. Bogus remarked. "The boys were usually behind in their studies because they worked in the fields and missed more school."

"So," Colette said, with a wink, "what's the reason they're behind today?"

"That's easy!" Drew said. "We're still busy working in the fields."

"What fields?" Lucia asked.

"Let's see," Drew said, counting on his fingers. "There's the football field, the baseball field, the soccer field, the track field, and we can't leave out the greatest field of battle, the basketball court."

"That's very clever, Drew," Ms. Bogus said. "Now that you've all had a chance see what life was like back in 1875, how do you think you would have liked living back then?"

Drew stood up first. "I think I would have liked it, Ms. B," he said. "I'm sure life was a little harder, but I think kids had it easier."

"Yeah!" several kids in the class shouted.

"There probably wasn't the kind of pressure put on kids in school like there is now," Drew added. "If you paced yourself, you could take your time learning stuff. But I would really miss video games."

"As my dad always says," Sarah said, "it's a great place to visit, but I wouldn't want to live there. Although, science was just about to take a big leap forward with the automobile, the airplane, and the Industrial Revolution just around the corner. That part would be cool."

"I like how brave the pioneers were," Lucia said. "To abandon everything you know, pack up a wagon with all of your belongings and go to a place you know nothing about takes real courage!"

"Aww!" Johnny said. "That's no harder than moving from a big city to some small town today—new schools, new jobs, new people to meet. I think that we could

do better at anything they did back then, because we're smarter than they were."

"Yeah!" a few kids said.

"You're crazy!" Willy cried. "My great, great grandfather, who was named Robert Williams, just like me, kept journals on his life growing up on a prairie farm. It was tough! He had to work just as hard as his dad. They had to make sure they had food to eat and a safe place to live. Nothing came easy, not even school. They learned stuff we will never learn now, and they knew how to do math the hard way, without a calculator."

"How many of you think it would be fun to travel the prairie today?" Ms. Bogus asked.

Everyone except Colette and Willy raised their hands.

"Very good!" Ms. Bogus said. "It's exciting to see that so many of you want to

know more. Let me show you what life on the prairie was like!"

The kids knew those words meant that they should clear off their desks. After doing so, they closed their eyes and listened to Ms. Bogus' monotone voice.

"First, there's the question of getting to the 1800s," she said. "But I'm sure the Jolly Jet can help us with that."

CHAPTER FOUR:

CONTAGIOUS!

Lucia suddenly felt a cool breeze on her face and smelled a familiar smell. She opened her eyes. They weren't in the schoolhouse anymore. They were on the Jolly Jet. She glanced out the window next to her and saw that they had already left Earth orbit.

"What's going on, Ms. B?" Drew asked. All the other kids piped in with lots of questions.

"Relax, everyone," Ms. Bogus said. "We're on the Jolly Jet, heading for the light bridge."

"Why?" Colette asked. "I thought this was supposed to be a trip to the late 1800s prairie."

"It still is, dear," Ms. Bogus replied. "But first, we have to get to the 1800s, and that's why we're on the Jolly Jet."

"How is that possible?" Sarah asked. "People can't travel through time."

"Well," Ms. Bogus answered, "people aren't supposed to be able to see the eight wonders of the world in less than a day, or travel to the Planet Mars in an hour, either, but most people don't have the Jolly Jet to take them wherever they believe they can go.

"Do you all believe we can visit the 1800s if we want to?" Ms. Bogus asked.

Every hand shot into the air.

"Do you all believe that anything is possible when we ride on the Jolly Jet?" Ms. Bogus asked.

Again, every hand went up.

"Children," Ms. Bogus said, "that is called faith. And faith in a belief or a cause will take you very far in life."

"Ms. B," Willy said, pointing to the lighted Fasten Your Seatbelt sign. "Does that mean what I think it means?"

"Yes, Willy," Ms. Bogus said. "It's the event horizon. We're entering the light bridge. Hang on!"

Ms. Bogus pushed a blue switch and a television monitor dropped from the ceiling at the front of the cabin. She quickly hit the *External View* switch and the monitor came to life, showing the Jolly Jet soaring through the center of the bright, triangular crystalline prism that made up the Light Bridge. The light around them divided into a magnificent array of colors.

"Wow!" Willy said, looking over at Drew. "This is sooooo contagious!"

CHAPTER FIVE:

THE JOLLY SCHOONER

The dazzling light on the monitor suddenly disappeared, replaced by an intense sun in a cloudless sky. Lucia realized she wasn't in the Jolly Jet anymore. Instead, she was sitting in a canvas-covered, horse-drawn wagon, bumping along a rutty trail. Tall grass and fragrant wildflowers grew abundantly on either side of the trail. The air smelled fresher than ever before.

All the children in the class were asking Ms. Bogus what happened.

"Children, children," Ms. Bogus said, trying to calm them down. "Don't worry. We're still on the Jolly Jet, but today it has transformed itself into a prairie schooner to take us across the plains."

"What's a prairie schooner?" Skylar asked.

"It was like a small moving truck of the 1800s," Willy replied. "It could support a lot of weight and transport heavy items over long distances. Without it, families wouldn't have been able to move all their stuff or carry supplies like chickens, oats, or seeds for planting when they traveled westward to make a new life."

"You sure know a lot about prairie life," Colette said, looking down at the plaid, ankle length dress she was wearing. "I guess that explains why we're dressed funny."

"Oh, my gosh!" Lucia said, eyeing her new clothes. "This is certainly not my style."

"I'm wearing suspenders!" Skylar said. "I never wear suspenders."

"But they're kind of fun to play with," Willy remarked, snapping Skylar's red suspenders against his white shirt.

"We're not dressed funny," Ms. Bogus said. "We're dressed in 1800s clothing so we blend in."

"Hey," Skylar asked, pointing toward a lone rider on horseback and a group of covered wagons behind him. "Who's that coming toward us, and what are all those wagons doing behind him?"

Ms. Bogus steered their horses toward the wagons.

"That's a wagon train," Willy said. "When the pioneers wanted to go west, they found other people that wanted to go, too. They all loaded their stuff into prairie schooners and traveled in a long, single line like a train. It was safer to travel together, and they could share the cost of supplies, too."

The man on horseback stopped alongside the Jolly Schooner. Dust swirled around him and his horse. He tilted his hat at Ms. Bogus.

"Howdy, Ma'am," he said. "You shouldn't be traveling out here alone. Would you like to join us? We're heading toward the Wyoming territory."

"That is so kind of you, sir," Ms. Bogus said. "We'd love to travel with you, ah, sir..."

"Cody, Bill Cody," the man declared. "Some people call me Buffalo Bill. I'm the wagonmaster for this here trip. Follow me, and I'll get a spot for you in line." He tilted his hat again and dug his spurs into his

horse, which bolted off toward the other wagons.

"That's Buffalo Bill Cody?" Sarah said with a gasp. "He was one of the most famous frontiersmen and Indian fighters in the Old West!"

"That's right!" Willy cried. "This trip is starting to look better and better!"

CHAPTER SIX:

INDIAN ATTACK

The sun was sinking on the western horizon when Buffalo Bill rode up to the Jolly Schooner again.

"Howdy, Miss," Buffalo Bill said, tilting his hat again. "We'll be setting up camp—"

"Injuns!" A frantic cry rang out from the first wagon in line.

Buffalo Bill raced to the front of the wagon train, shouting instructions all the way. The train quickly broke into two sections that came together to form an overlapping circle.

"Women and children—out of the wagons!" Buffalo Bill ordered. "Get down in the center!"

"Come on, class," Ms. Bogus said. "Hurry!" She climbed off the wagon and ran to the center of the circle, gathering the children around her.

Willy lagged behind, watching the men ready their rifles and swords. "Don't shoot unless I say so," Buffalo Bill shouted. "There are some friendly Injuns in these parts."

"Man," Willy said, walking up and standing by his crouching classmates, "is this the coolest thing, or what?"

"Willy, are you nuts?" Sarah asked. "This is no joke. Get down before those Indians scalp you or something."

"They're not going to scalp anyone," Willy said. "My great, great grandfather wrote in his journal about the Indians in this part of Iowa. He said that by 1846 there were mostly friendly Indians in these parts. Besides, Buffalo Bill Cody will protect us!"

ZING!

An arrow zoomed past Willy's head and stuck in the side of the wagon. Ms. Bogus threw Willy to the ground.

"Fire!" Buffalo Bill shouted. The girls covered their ears as gunshots rang out all around them. The battle raged for just a few terrifying minutes until the Indians turned suddenly and galloped away, except for one. He turned toward the kids and shot a flaming arrow at the Jolly Schooner before racing away on his spotted pony.

Instead of sticking in the Jolly Schooner, the arrow ricocheted off the side and landed in back of another family's wagon.

Willy, Drew, and Skylar jumped up and ran to the wagon where the fire was quickly spreading.

"Grab the bonnet out of the jockey box on the side of the wagon!" Willy yelled. He pointed at a canvas wagon cover lying in a wooden box hanging on the side of the wagon. Skylar and Drew threw it over the fire, scrambled into the wagon, and jumped up and down on the canvas until the fire was out.

"Thank you so much!" a woman shouted, over the noise of a crate of squawking chickens attached to the other side of the wagon. Buffalo Bill appeared at her side.

"Boys," Buffalo Bill said, "you were brave and kind to help out a stranger like that. It's an honor to have you on this trip."

He turned toward the women. "Mrs. Williams, Miss Bogus, we're setting up camp here tonight, so you need to get your horses bedded down. Also, I'm pretty sure that the chuck wagon cook would appreciate any help he can get." He tipped his hat and swaggered away.

"So much for them being friendly Indians, Willy," Lucia said.

"Hey," Willy said, "I said my great, great grandfather wrote that there were *mostly* friendly Indians in these parts. I guess these were the few that weren't," he added with a frown. "What was that woman's name again?"

"Williams," Lucia said. "Why?"

"No reason," Willy said.

"She seems very nice," Lucia remarked, as the woman's two children ran up to her. The girl hugged her mother. The boy stood by her side with a book in his hand. The word "Journal" was printed on the front.

"Robert," the woman said to her son. "Bed down the horses." Robert nodded and began to loosen the harnesses.

Drew walked up to Willy and Lucia. "Do either of you know how to bed down horses?" he asked.

CHAPTER SEVEN:

JOHNNYCAKES AND BUTTER

Robert Williams finished his chores before most of the other children. He grabbed his sister and strolled over to the Jolly Schooner, where Lucia was showing Willy, Drew, and Skylar how to care for the horses. Sarah and Colette were helping the chuck wagon cook prepare dinner.

"Hi! My name is Robert, and this is my sister, Sally," he said. "Thank you for saving our wagon."

"You're welcome," Willy said. "I'm Willy, and this is Lucia, Drew, and Skylar."

"Hi," Robert said, looking at Drew and Skylar. "You two are twins, huh?"

"Yeah," Skylar said. "But you can tell us apart by..."

"Your eye color," Robert said. He looked at the other children in the class sitting on the ground nearby. "Are you from an orphanage?" he asked.

"Not exactly," Willy replied. He quickly changed the subject. "Where are you headed?"

"Everyone else here is going to Wyoming," Robert explained, "but we're just going back to Grover Creek, Iowa. We have a farm there.

"In fact," he added, "this is probably going to be one of the last wagon trains going through Grover Creek, because the railroad will have the tracks to Grover Creek finished any day now."

"That's right!" Sally said. "Then people will start taking the train to get there. Grover Creek is going to have a big shindig with fireworks and all sorts of fun when the railroad workers are done. You ought to come!"

Colette sat quietly in an old wooden chair, **agitating** the mixture in the butter churner in front of her. The cook, Charlie, had skimmed the fatty cream off the top of a container of cow's milk and put it in the churn for her. The stirring would whip the cream into frothy whipped cream, and finally into butter.

Sarah was a mess. Her tousled hair and green dress were caked with a light coating of yellow cornmeal. She and Charlie were making fresh Johnnycakes.

"How long have you been making Johnnycakes?" Sarah asked, wiping cornmeal from her hands onto her apron.

"This recipe," Charlie said, "of cornmeal, sugar, and hot water has been handed down for generations in my family. If you've never had Johnnycakes, you're in for a treat. You'll see what I mean once we fry them in butter!"

Charlie had been watching Colette. "You are a very persistent young lady," he said. "You haven't stop churning since you started. Let me take a look and see how you're coming."

Colette stopped and Charlie opened the churn cover. "Oh, yes!" he said. "This is perfect. Good job."

"Thank you," Colette said, flexing her cramped fingers. She knew the discomfort would **dissipate** in a few minutes.

"Okay," Charlie said, as he poured the mixture in the churn through a piece of cheesecloth covering a large bowl. "It's time to make some great-tasting butter."

"I thought that's what I was doing," Colette said.

"Churnin' is just the first step," Charlie said. "Then we separate the buttermilk from the butter by passing it through the cheesecloth. I use the buttermilk for baking." Sure enough, a large clump of butter sat on the cheesecloth when he finished pouring.

Charlie picked up the cheesecloth and ran cool water over the butter.

"Why do you do that?" Sarah asked.

"To wash off the rest of the buttermilk," Charlie replied. "It can cause the butter to spoil." He scooped the butter into a smaller bowl and stirred in some salt for flavoring.

"Since you did all the hard work, Colette, you get first taste," Charlie said.

Colette leaned forward and sampled the butter. Her eyes grew wide and her lips turned up into a smile. "Oh, my!" Colette said. "That's the best-tasting butter I've ever had!"

"Can I try the stew I helped make?" Sarah asked.

"Why, sure," Charlie replied, scooping up a spoonful. "You're going to love this!"

"It's delicious!" Sarah said. "The meat is so tender. Is it chicken?"

"No," Charlie said. "We need all our chickens for eggs. That's rattlesnake stew, dear, the best in the whole darn country, if I do say so myself. It's tasty, huh?"

Sarah gulped. "Y-y-yes, sir!"

CHAPTER EIGHT:

COCK-A-DOODLE-DOO

COCK-A-DOODLE-DOO!
COCK-A-DOODLE-DOO!
Willy kicked off his blanket and jumped up. "What in the world is that?" he shouted. Drew and Skylar sat up a few seconds after Willy. Lucia rolled over and rubbed her eyes, while Colette and Sarah continued to sleep.

"That's Jasper," said Robert, standing behind the kids. "He's our rooster. His crowing means it's time to get

up and get our chores done before Charlie makes breakfast."

"But," Drew said, "the sun's not even up yet. Can't we sleep a little longer?"

"Nope!" Robert said. "We've got to gather some eggs for Charlie, feed the horses and the chickens, and milk the cows, because as soon as breakfast is over, we'll be moving again."

"Man," Drew said, "This is not turning out like our last two field trips. They were more like vacations."

"What's a vacation?" Robert asked.

"It's when you take time off from work and chores and go have fun," Skylar said. "Vacations are awesome."

"What does 'awesome' mean?" Robert asked.

"Umm!" Skylar said. "It means that something is fun, or enjoyable."

"Oh, I get it," Robert said. "So, would I be right if I said that school was *not* awesome?"

"Yes!" Skylar said with a nod.

"Awesome!" Robert said.

Robert picked up a bucket and was about to gather some eggs when he suddenly remembered he had helpers. "Drew," he asked, "can you and Skylar take those two canvas bags right there, fill them with oats from the bag on the other side of the wagon, and put them on the horses? Willy, will you help me gather the eggs for Charlie?"

Willy was still to sleepy to complain. "Sure," he said, "lead the way."

Drew and Skylar just looked at each other. "He wanted us to do what?" Drew asked.

Lucia jumped out from under her blanket. "Come on, city boys," she said. "I'll show you how to feed the horses."

CHAPTER NINE:

RIVER RIDE

By noon, the sun was bearing down on the thin ribbon of white wagons as the wagon train wove its way along the unmarked trail toward Grover Creek. "It is sooooo hot," Johnny said. "I wish we were back in the Jolly Jet."

"Hey, my friend," Willy said, wiping the sweat off his brow with the back of his hand. "I thought you said you could do anything better than the people in the 1800s. Well, this is what they lived in day in and day out.   There was no air conditioning to cool them down!"

"I was wrong," Johnny admitted. "If they can survive this kind of heat, they're better than me.   All I want is some air conditioning, with no Indians, no rattlesnake stew, and no sleeping on the ground."

"I liked the rattlesnake stew," Colette said.

"I did, too," Willy added. "It tasted like chicken."   Sarah shuddered at the memory of rattlesnake stew.

Ms. Bogus heard the children talking. She flipped open a small door on the seat beside her. The instrument panel from the Jolly Jet was hidden inside and easily **accessible** for emergencies.   She pressed a button, and cool air rushed up to fill the canvas bonnet over the wagon. It poured out of tiny holes down onto the children.

"That should cool you down," Ms. Bogus said.

"Thank you, Ms. B!" the kids shouted.

The wagon train had slowed to cross a fast-moving river. Buffalo Bill rode up next to Ms. Bogus. "Howdy, ma'am," he said, tilting his hat again. "Be careful crossing the river. It's unusually high for this time of year, but so far all the wagons have made it across." He looked at the Jolly Schooner. "Your wagon is shorter than most," he observed, "so you may take on some water. You children need to grab something and hold on tight!" He moved on to the next wagon behind them.

"Are we going to make it across, Ms. B?" Sarah asked.

"Sure, dear," Ms. Bogus said. "The Jolly Schooner can make it anywhere."

Ms. Bogus pulled on the reins to slow the horses down as they rolled into the swift current. The children watched the Williams' wagon reach the other shore.

"Robert and Sally made it safely across," Willy said, with a sigh of relief.

Another wagon pulled alongside the Jolly Schooner. "Comin' through," their driver shouted. His wheels almost touched the Schooner. "Sorry, but I've got to get to the other side fast. My wife's with child and she just went into labor!"

Just as Ms. Bogus waved him by, the man's wagon wheel struck a boulder hidden under the water, tipping his wagon toward the Jolly Schooner. The wagon's brake lever smacked Ms. Bogus in the head, knocking her unconscious. The wagon slid further into the Jolly Schooner, pushing it into deeper water. The man managed to get his horses to pull his wagon away, but it was too late. The Jolly Schooner was heading down the river toward a set of foaming white rapids!

CHAPTER TEN:

OVER THE EDGE

Drew and Willy quickly moved Ms. B to a seat inside the Jolly Schooner as it swept around a bend in the river. Lucia grabbed the reins to control the horses, but wasn't having much success.

"I can't control the horses!" Lucia shouted. "We're heading for the rapids! If anyone has any bright ideas, speak up now!"

"Hey!" Skylar yelled, as he looked at Ms. B's instrument panel. "You can't control the horses, because the auto navigation button is pressed in. In other words, the Jolly Schooner is controlling the horses. If this really is our Jolly Jet instrument panel, this thing has got to be able to fly. I just have to find the right button!"

ROOAAARRR!

"Is that what I think it is?" Willy asked.

"It sounds like a..." Drew started to say, as the edge of a massive waterfall appeared ahead, "...waterfall! Skylar, you've got to hurry or this field trip is going to end real fast!"

"I'm looking!" Skylar shouted, "but there are a bunch of switches that have the lettering worn off. They're hard to read with the sunlight shining on them."

ROOOAAARRRR!

The children started screaming as they approached the edge. "Hang on!" Willy shouted, as the Jolly Schooner slipped over the drop-off.

The wagon plummeted toward the river below. Suddenly, Willy could feel a power in the Jolly Schooner that wasn't there before. The wheels turned to the side like wings. The Schooner lifted out of its freefall, flew over the river, and banked around toward the shore.

Drew grabbed Skylar in a bear hug. "Little brother, you did it!" he shouted. "You saved our lives. How did you find the button?"

"When we went over the edge," Skylar replied, "the sun wasn't shining on the panel anymore so I could read the lettering. I just pressed the one that said, *Engine Start.*"

"And by the way," Skylar added, "watch the 'little brother' stuff. I was only born two minutes after you."

"Well," Lucia said, as the Jolly Schooner soared over the riverbank below, "you had better get us down before we scare all those people who have never seen an airplane in their lives!"

Skylar pressed the *Land* button and the wagon set down smoothly in a field of wildflowers. "There you go, Lucia," Skylar said. "I also took the horses off auto navigation. You can control them now."

"Ohhh!" Ms. Bogus moaned, rubbing her head. "What happened? I thought we were crossing the river."

"We took a slight detour from the wagon train, Ms. B," Willy explained, "but now that you're awake, I'm sure you can get us back on track!"

CHAPTER ELEVEN:

HAVE YOU EVER HEARD OF A UFO?

Lucia drove the horses, while Ms. Bogus sat on the seat next to her. "Are you okay, Ms. B?" Lucia asked.

"Yes, dear," Ms. Bogus replied, "but I'll be better once the throbbing in my head goes away."

"You got hit pretty hard with that brake handle," Lucia said. "I'm surprised you're not seeing two of everything."

"Really?" Ms. Bogus asked. "And I was just going to ask you the name of your twin sister sitting next to you."

"Ha!" Willy said. "Ms. Bogus made a joke! That means it's time to tell a couple of knock-knock jokes."

"Knock-knock," Willy said.

Everyone was quiet. Willy just waited. "Okay," Lucia said, "who's there?"

"Water!" Willy answered.

"Water who?" Lucia asked.

"Water fall we almost took," Willy said. Several kids laughed.

"I've got a better one," Colette said. "I thought of it while I watched Drew milk Robert's cow this morning. Knock-knock!"

"Who's there?" Drew asked.

"Cows!" Colette said.

"Cows who?" Drew asked.

"Cows go 'moo,' not 'who,' silly!" Colette said.

Everyone but Willy laughed. "Why is it that you guys laugh at everyone's jokes except mine?" he asked.

"That's easy to answer," Lucia said. "Your jokes..."

BANG! BANG!

Lucia stopped talking as she heard the gunshots. Just ahead of them, two cowboys were trying to round up a small herd of cattle.

"What are they doing?" Sarah asked.

"Cattle rustling!" Willy said.

"Stay calm!" Ms. Bogus ordered.

"Ms. B," Drew said, "we can't let those guys steal that cattle. It isn't right."

The cowboys saw the Jolly Schooner and galloped toward it. "Don't go anywhere, Lucia," Skylar said.

The men approached them with their guns drawn. "Well, looky here, Tyler. We done got us a bunch of children," one of the rustlers said.

Drew leaned over and whispered something to Skylar.

"Hey, boy," Tyler said. "Don't you speak unless I tell you to, you hear?"

"Yes, sir," Drew said. "I was just wondering if you knew what a UFO is."

"A what, boy?" Tyler asked.

Drew nodded at his brother. Skylar pressed *Auto Navigation*, then *Engine Start*. The Jolly Schooner jolted into the air above the men, scaring their horses. Tyler's horse started to buck, throwing him to the ground. It galloped away as fast as its muscular legs could carry it. Tyler's gun flew out of his hand into a deep, thorny thicket.

Tyler's partner managed to keep his horse under control. He aimed his gun at the Jolly Schooner. Just as he was about to pull the trigger, the horses spun the wagon around, knocking him to the ground. The two cattle rustlers scrambled to their feet and escaped into the trees.

"That was pretty smart, Drew!" Willy said. "You're on a roll today, too, Skylar," he added.

"Thanks," Skylar said, bringing the wagon back down to the ground. "Here come a couple more cowboys," he said. "Let's hope these are good guys for a change."

"Howdy, folks," one of the men said. "Have you seen anyone trying to run off with some cattle?"

"Yes, we did, sir," Drew said. "Something spooked them and they ran off that a way," he said, pointing in the direction the men had run.

"Thank you kindly," the man said. "Where are you heading?" he asked.

"Grover Creek," Willy said. "Do you know how far we are from it?"

"Not far at all," the man said. "You have about five miles to go. Thanks again," the man repeated, as he rode off after the rustlers.

"Why are we going to Grover Creek?" Skylar asked.

"They're having a big shindig to celebrate the railroad coming to town," Willy said. "I know Ms. B wouldn't want to pass up a chance to have some fun. Isn't that right, Ms. B?"

"I just hope it's relaxing," Ms. Bogus said. "I think we've all had enough excitement for one day!"

CHAPTER TWELVE:

HOME SWEET HOME

The Jolly Schooner lumbered into Grover Creek in mid-afternoon. Willy recognized several families in the wagon train coming out of the County Surveyor's Office. They were looking into the government's offer to give out parcels of land to families who agreed to settle there.

Ms. Bogus stepped off the Jolly Schooner after Lucia pulled it to a stop in front of the town's only hotel. It was right next to the general store. "Class, I'm going to see if I can get some rooms for us," she said. "I'll be right back."

"Except for being muddier," Skylar remarked, "this town looks just like Walnut Hill back at the Living History Farm."

"Yeah!" Colette said. "But the people look a lot more rugged."

Ms. Bogus hurried out of the hotel with a smile on her face. She held up her forefinger as if to say, "just wait a few minutes more," and slipped inside the general store.

Suddenly, Robert and Sally bolted out of the store entrance. "You guys made it!" Robert shouted. "We thought you were goners for sure when we saw your wagon heading for the waterfall."

"Naw," Willy said. "We made it out okay, but it was a little scary for a minute or two!"

Ms. Bogus walked out of the general store arm in arm with Robert and Sally's mom. "Class, the hotel has room for all but six of us, so Mrs. Williams here has been kind enough to allow six of you to stay at her home."

Willy's eyes were as big as walnuts. "Are you okay, Willy?" Ms. Bogus asked.

Willy just nodded his head.

"Okay, then," Ms. Bogus said. "We'll let your group stay with them. Is that okay with you?"

Willy nodded his head again.

Ms. Bogus turned to Mrs. Williams. "Thank you so much for your kindness."

"It's a pleasure," Mrs. Williams said. "We'll show the children how a prairie farm is run, don't worry.

"This will be a great learning experience for you, children," she continued, "and I'm sure Robert and Sally will enjoy your stay. Lucia, just follow us in your wagon."

CHAPTER THIRTEEN:

THIS IS A WORKING FARM, BOYS!

Mr. Williams left the field he was clearing to meet his wife and children near the house. "What have we here?" he said, pointing to the wagon full of kids.

"This is Willy, Drew, Skylar, Lucia, Sarah, and Colette," Sally said. "Mama said they could stay with us for a few days. Can they, Papa?"

"Fine with me," Mr. Williams replied. "I can use a hand around here."

"You take the boys," Mrs. Williams said, "and show them how to do some sodbusting. The girls will help me get dinner going."

Drew removed Colette's wheelchair from under the wagon where it had been stored. Willy helped him lift Colette into the chair. She just stared at it—it didn't look like her modern wheelchair.

"I'm not used to a hard wooden seat," she whispered to Drew. "This may hurt after a while."

As if reading Colette's mind, Mrs. Williams said, "Colette, tonight after dinner, Sally and I will make a nice padded pillow for you to sit on."

"Thank you!" Colette said with a big smile.

"What's sodbusting?" Skylar asked Willy, as they chased each other on the way to the field.

"It's when you clear prairie land," Willy explained. "From what my great,

great grandfather wrote," he continued, "it isn't fun."

"This is a working farm, boys," Mr. Williams said. "You are more than welcome to stay with us, but every person has to do his fair share of work. As my Pappy used to say, if you expect to eat, you have to move your feet." He pointed to the sodbusting plow.

It looked like a gigantic wooden lawn mower. The thick wood handles curved backward. The reins fastened over the driver's shoulders, and a plow horse pulled it. The plowing end consisted of a wide, flat blade attached to a piece of thick, beveled hardwood.

"I can promise you, this will be hard work," Mr. Williams said, smiling. "Son, take Skylar and show him how to take care of the horses before dinner, while Willy and Drew take a try at sodbusting."

"Okay, Papa," Robert said. "We'll come back when we finish." Robert pulled Skylar back toward the wagons. "This must be your lucky day," he whispered, "because taking care of horses is a lot easier than sodbusting."

Mr. Williams wrapped the long reins over Willy's shoulders. If my great, great grandfather can do this, Willy thought, I can, too!

"Bessie will pull you," Mr. Williams said. "Your job is to keep your weight on the sodbuster so it digs into the soil and cuts a good layer of sod out. The hard part is keeping it upright while you're trying to steer Bessie and hold the plow steady. Moving your weight to one side of the plow will move it in that direction.

"When you want Bessie to go, say, 'pull, girl,'" Mr. Williams continued. "When you want her to stop, say, 'whoa, girl.' If you need her to back up, say, 'back, girl.' Keep her as straight as you can, but make sure you slightly overlap the area that's already done."

Willy nodded his head. Sounds a bit like skateboarding with someone pulling you, he thought. "Okay," he said. "Here goes nothing. Pull, girl!"

Bessie started walking at an easy pace. Everything seemed to be going fine until Willy noticed that the plow was moving to the left. He leaned his weight to the right, but put too much pressure on the corner of the plow. It dug too deeply into the soil and popped out from under the sod as it fell to the ground. Bessie kept moving, dragging Willy off the plow and through the prairie grass. "Whoa," he cried, but the horse kept moving. Then Willy shouted, "Whoa, girl!" And Bessie came to a stop.

As he stood up, Willy heard Mr. Williams and Drew laughing heartily. I'll show them, he thought. "Back, girl!" Bessie backed up to the plow as Willy wrestled it upright. He straightened his reins, centered his weight, and gripped the plow handles. The laughter behind him had stopped.

CHAPTER FOURTEEN:

DIRT SURFING

"Pull, girl!" Willy said, as Bessie started off again. This time he went twice as far as he had the first time before the plow began to move over.

"You got it, Willy!" Drew sang out. "Keep it going. It's just like skateboarding. Shift your weight easy."

"What is that—skateboarding?" Mr. Williams asked.

"Uh, uh!" Drew searched for an answer. "Back east, we put wheels on boards and roll them down hills. You control your direction with your weight on the edges of the board."

Mr. Williams took his hat off and scratched his head. "Well, I'll be darned. What will they think of next?"

You wouldn't believe me if I told you, Drew thought.

Suddenly, Bessie stopped and reared up, kicking her front feet. Willy saw the striped rattlesnake on the ground in front of her just before he fell off the plow. Bessie sprinted through the field, dragging Willy behind her.

"OW, OW, OWW!" Willy shouted with every bump. He heard a gunshot ring out just as he untangled the first loop of reins from around his shoulders. He had just pulled the other rein over his head when Bessie leaped over a mound of dirt. Willy sailed through the air. He tumbled to the ground and rolled several times, stopping inches away from a jagged boulder. One more roll and he would have smacked his head right into it.

"Willy! Willy!" Drew shouted, running up to his friend. He rolled Willy over. "Are you okay?"

Willy slowly opened his eyes. "Come on, pardner," he said. "You don't think a little bumpy ride is going to stop me, do ya? I got more bruises falling off the first skateboard you gave me."

Mr. Williams caught up to them. He touched the **laceration** on Billy's cheek. "You'll be alright," he said, reaching out his hand. "Come on boy, we need to find Bessie before she ends up in the next county."

As they trudged back to the barn, Willy could feel every bruise on his aching body. "How was I doing until that rattler came along?" he asked.

Mr. Williams put his arm around Willy's shoulder. "Willy," he said, "you are about as stubborn as Robert is, which is my

way of saying you did good, son!
Real good!"

Willy's chest swelled up and his
shoulders straightened.

CHAPTER FIFTEEN:

A SAW IS A MAN'S BEST FRIEND

After dinner, Willy patted his stomach. "Mrs. Williams, that was a great meal. I could live on the fresh bread and butter forever! And that chicken was even better than the rattlesnake stew we had yesterday."

"Thank you," Mrs. Williams said, "but some of the credit goes to Sarah, Colette, Lucia, and Sally. They did a wonderful job helping me."

Mrs. Williams turned toward her husband. "Now," she said, "you boys can retire to the porch, while we ladies clean up the kitchen."

Willy gave a "ha, ha, we don't have to work!" look to Lucia. She stuck her tongue out at him. Drew and Skylar just smiled as they left the cabin.

The boys followed Mr. Williams off the porch and toward the barn. "Did you see that?" Drew whispered to Skylar and Willy. "I could get used to this stuff where the girls have to work and we men get to relax."

Mr. Williams laughed. "Drew, this is a farm. There is no such thing as relaxing until it's Sunday. We work from the moment our feet hit the floor until we put them back under the sheets.

"See that log?" Mr. Williams asked, pointing to a large tree trunk sitting between two X-shaped crossbeam supports.

"We need to turn that log into firewood before dark."

"I think Willy has taken enough of a beating today," Mr. Williams said. "It's time to see what you twins are made of." He lifted a saw that was as long as he was tall, onto the log. "This is a cross cut saw," he explained. "It takes two people to cut with it." Mr. Williams and Robert gave the boys a short demonstration on how to use the saw.

Skylar and Drew grabbed either end of the saw and began pulling it back and forth. They kept it up until they were about halfway through the log. Skylar began to breathe hard. As he pulled back on his handle, the blade stopped, causing him to lose his grip and fall backwards.

Mr. Williams snickered as the boys started to laugh. "You okay there, boy?" Mr. Williams asked.

"Yeah!" Skylar said. "What did I do wrong?"

"See the way Drew has his feet positioned apart front to back?" Mr. Williams said. "You need to stand like that. Now, try it again."

Skylar positioned himself properly and started cutting. "Oh, man," he said. "This makes it a lot easier. I wish you would've told me this before."

"What?" Mr. Williams joked, "and miss that great fall of yours?"

CHAPTER SIXTEEN:

FAMILY TIES

The next day, after helping Robert finish his chores, Mr. Williams and the boys went into town to help prepare the schoolhouse field for the big shindig. Willy swung a scythe over the top of the grass, mowing down a three-foot section in one swipe. "Wow!" he said, "if this wasn't so much work, this could be fun."

Willy was happy to be working side-by-side with Mr. Williams and Robert. The field was almost ready. Willy shook his sore arms and took another swipe.

Lucia appeared, carrying a pitcher. "Would you like a glass of cool lemonade, Willy?" she asked.

"You bet," Willy replied. Setting the scythe down, he wiped his forehead with the back of his arm. "Are you having a good time?"

"Yes and no," Lucia said, handing Willy his drink. "These dresses are so stiff, and I feel like I've got to be prim and proper at all times.

"But I really like Mr. and Mrs. Williams," she added. "Isn't it funny that they have the same last name as you? And I remember you saying that your dad is Robert Williams III, which means that your great, great grandfather, who wrote those journals, was named Robert, too." Lucia looked over at Robert swinging his scythe. Willy followed her gaze. "It must be

incredible to meet your family from long ago."

Willy smiled. "Has anyone else figured it out?"

"No," Lucia said, "not that I know of, except maybe Ms. B."

"I'd like to keep it that way," Willy said.

Lucia nodded. "I understand," she said. "Mrs. Williams is going to take Sally back to the farm to get ready for tonight, but Colette, Sarah, and I told her we wanted to walk back with you guys. We'll be over at the general store whenever you are ready."

CHAPTER SEVENTEEN:

BAD GUYS!

Willy, Drew, and Skylar walked up the middle of the main street though town toward the general store.

They stopped in front of the Grover Creek Bank, when they saw Lucia, Sarah, and Colette coming toward them with water balloons.

"I done told ya da war wasn't over yet, Willy," Lucia shouted, as Sarah and Colette disappeared among the buildings. "We're gonna finish it here and now."

The boys split up. Willy grinned as he dove behind a water trough near the bank. Suddenly, the bank's doors flew open and two masked men raced out. One carried a large leather bag. The other man wore a brown hat and carried a fancy cane.

The man in the hat touched the hooked handle of the cane to his hat, as they both mounted their horses. "Thanks for your generous contribution to our retirement fund, folks."

Lucia stood in the middle of the street, frozen in place. The water balloons dropped from her hands. One of them broke while the other rolled slowly toward the bank.

"Tom and Harry Croacher!" the sheriff yelled from the doorway of the general store. "Throw that leather bag to the ground—right now!"

The two men spun their horses around to face the sheriff, who had his hand on the gun in his holster. The fancy cane tumbled to the ground.

"He means business, Tom," said Harry, the man with the leather bag. He dropped the bag in the dirt and slowly climbed down from his horse.

Willy was crouched close to where Tom Croacher sat on his horse. He saw Tom reaching for his gun. Willy knew he had to get Lucia out of way in case any shots rang out.

RAATTTLLE!

Willy saw the rattler out of the corner of his eye. It had slithered out from under the bank walkway. He noticed the cane near his feet. He slowly reached over and picked up the cane by its tip.

"No!" Willy shouted. He leaped to his feet and whipped the hooked end of the cane under the rattler. With his other hand, he scooped up the balloon and flung it at Tom Croacher.

SPLASH!

The balloon hit Tom's horse in the neck. The horse reared up, knocking Tom to the ground.

Harry spun around, and Willy whipped the rattler off the cane right at him.

The angry rattler landed hard against Harry's shoulder, and embedded its teeth into his chest. AAIIIIEEEEEE! Harry screamed.

Willy ran past the two men and grabbed Lucia. He pulled her across the street between two buildings.

Harry squirmed on the ground, trying to unhook the snake from his chest. The sheriff and two deputies raced over to the two men, forcing their hands behind

their backs and handcuffing them. "That's it for you, Croacher boys!" the sheriff shouted.

CHAPTER EIGHTEEN:

TIME TO GO!

After the shindig, the kids walked slowly back to the farm.

"That was really fun," Sally said.

"Yeah!" Skylar said. "I had a good time."

"I wish you didn't have to leave tonight," Robert said, "but at least I've got braggin' rights."

"Bragging rights?" Colette said. "For what?"

"I had the guy who helped capture some bank robbers living in my house,"

Robert said. "That makes me tops in the eyes of my friends."

"How are you doing, Lucia?" Sarah asked.

"I'm okay," Lucia said, "but if it wasn't for Willy, I don't know what would have happened. I don't think I've ever been more afraid in my life. I've never seen anyone with guns except on TV."

"What's TV?" Sally asked, as all the kids looked at Lucia for an explanation of her slip of the tongue.

"Oh," Lucia said, brushing her hand through the air. "It means 'theatrical villains.' My mom takes me to see lots of plays at the theater."

Willy laughed. "Yeah," he said, "her mom loves going to the theater."

Ms. Bogus was waiting in the Jolly Schooner with the rest of the class when they arrived at the farm. They all said goodbye to Mr. and Mrs. Williams, Robert, and Sally.

Willy was the last one in line. Mrs. Williams gave him a big hug with tears in her eyes. Mr. Williams grabbed his hand firmly and shook it.

"You've been a big help around here, Willy," Mr. Williams said. "We're all going to miss you. I don't think I've ever met a boy your age as brave as you. I bet you come from good stock."

"I'm told I do, sir," Willy said, smiling.

"You take care of yourself," Sally said.

Willy nodded.

As Robert shook Willy's hand, he said, "The next time you visit, you're going to show me that skateboarding thing you told my dad about."

"I'll do that," Willy said. "It would be my pleasure."

EPILOGUE

After returning to the schoolhouse at the Living History Farm, the kids discussed whether they had really visited the prairie or had just imagined it. Ms. B would not tell them one way or the other. "You each have to decide that for yourself," she said.

By the time Willy got home, he was starting to doubt it ever happened. He grabbed a box off the top shelf in his closet and put it on his bed. He rummaged through it until he found what he was looking for—the four journals written by his great, great grandfather, Robert. They were bound together with a thick rubber band.

He hadn't looked at them for about two years. He thumbed through each one until he stopped at the page that had been buried deep in his memory. As he ran his fingers over the page, he read it out loud.

"What a day! Willy helped the sheriff stop some bank robbers before the town's big shindig, and he kept Lucia from getting hurt. But he had to head back east after the party. I don't know if I'll ever meet up with him again. I hope so, because he felt like the brother I never had. He was awesome!"

THE END

ABOUT THE AUTHOR

 Carole Marsh is an author and publisher who has written many works of fiction and non-fiction for young readers. She travels throughout the United States and around the world to research her books. In 1979 Carole Marsh was named Communicator of the Year for her corporate communications work with major national and international corporations.

Marsh is the founder and CEO of Gallopade International, established in 1979. Today, Gallopade International is widely recognized as a leading source of educational materials for every state and many countries. Marsh and Gallopade were recipients of the 2004 Teachers' Choice Award. Marsh has written more than 50 Carole Marsh Mysteries™. In 2007, she was named Georgia Author of the Year. Years ago, her children, Michele and Michael, were the original characters in her mystery books. Today, they continue the Carole Marsh Books tradition by working at Gallopade. By adding grandchildren Grant and Christina as new mystery characters, she has continued the tradition for a third generation.

Ms. Marsh welcomes correspondence from her readers. You can e-mail her at fanclub@gallopade.com, visit carolemarshmysteries.com, or write to her in care of Gallopade International, P.O. Box 2779, Peachtree City, Georgia, 30269 USA.

BOOK CLUB
TALK ABOUT IT!

1. Would you like to meet a grandparent
    when they were the same age as you are
    today? What do you think that would be
    like?

2. Why did it bother Sarah to eat rattlesnake
    stew? Would that bother you?

3. People who lived on the prairie had a lot
    of hard work to do. What's your least
    favorite chore? Why?

4. Mr. Williams was confused when Drew
    mentioned skateboarding. Which
    activities or inventions of today do you
    think would seem the most outrageous to
    someone on the prairie?

5. Rattlesnakes and robbers were two very
    big dangers to pioneers. What other
    things do you think were dangerous on a
    trip across the frontier?

6. Why do you think the opening up of the railroad was so exciting for the cowboys?

7. How do you think the Native Americans felt when all the pioneers came through on the wagon trains?

8. The students in Ms. Bogus' class felt silly in pioneer clothing. If you're a girl, how would you feel if you had to wear a long dress and a bonnet every day? If you're a boy, how would you feel about those suspenders?

9. What do you think would be the best thing about living on a prairie schooner? What would be the worst?

10. Willy's family traveled on the prairie. What do you know about the historic times your grandparents or great grandparents lived in? Would you want to travel back to their times?

BOOK CLUB
BRING IT TO LIFE

1. Can you imagine life on a wagon train? There would be hard work, but there must have been some fun, too! Write a journal entry about a day on a wagon train.

2. The students were frightened when the flaming arrow came flying past them during the Indian attack. Make your own flaming arrows with red, yellow, and orange construction paper and pipe cleaners!

3. Pretend you've been on the prairie for weeks and weeks. Write a poem about how you think you would be feeling.

4. Imagine you're an animal living on the prairie. What do you think it would be like to see all those people traveling across the land where you live? Gather in groups of three or four and write a short skit pretending to be prairie animals. Perform these skits for your classmates!

PRAIRIE TRIVIA

1. When a wagon needed to cross a river, the
    pioneers had two options. They could drive
    across the river or float across if the water was
    too deep.

2. Pioneers traveled across the frontier in *wagon
    trains*. They were like small communities
    moving across the plains with food, tools, and
    elected leaders.

3. When people in California found
    gold, pioneers from all
    over America traveled
    across the country to try
    to find gold themselves.
    This was known as the
    Gold Rush.

4. Kids on the prairie found many things to do for
    fun. For example, after a pig was slaughtered
    for food, kids would play catch with the pig's
    bladder! It's just like a balloon!

5. There wasn't much space to carry food on covered wagons, so the men had to hunt for food frequently.

6. Pioneers slept right inside their wagons. There were small mattresses under the canvas where the whole family would huddle together.

7. Sometimes prairie farmhouses were built right into the hillsides! This saved wood and kept the families safe and cool. The roof was made of grass, too!

8. If a woman in a wagon train was going to have a baby, her family would ask people in the other wagons if a doctor was traveling in the group. A lot of babies were born in the wagon trains!

9. Everyone on the prairie had an important job. Kids even younger than you learned to build, sew, hunt, and cook.

10. During the long journey across the
    country, the pioneers entertained
    themselves by making things. Girls
    learned how to knit or sew, and made
    clothes and dolls. Boys learned how to
    build and whittle wood into toys and
    tools.

11. Going to school was impossible on the wagon
    train, so parents taught their children to read
    and write in the back of the wagon!

12. The wagons in the train were known as covered
    wagons, Conestoga wagons, or prairie
    schooners.

GLOSSARY

accessible: capable of being entered or reached

agitate: to shake or move back and forth; or to disturb

beveled: being cut to create a slope

boisterous: rough and noisy; rowdy

dissipate: to cause to go in all sorts of directions

embed: set securely or deeply

laceration: a cut or tear on the body tissue

lumber: to move along slowly and heavily

mill: to move around continuously in an aimless way

monotone: an unchanging tone of voice

plummet: to drop or fall very fast

shindig: a party or lively gathering

POP QUIZ

1. What was the name of the town where the Living History Farm was located?

2. What year was the town supposed to represent?

3. What saved the Jolly Schooner from going over the waterfall?

4. What animal bit Harry on the chest?

5. How were schoolhouses of the 1800s different from your school?

6. Who was Buffalo Bill?

7. How did Willy help save Sally and Robert's wagon?

8. What was the name of the plow horse that dragged Willy through the grass while he was sodbusting?

SCAVENGER HUNT

Want to have some fun? Let's go on a scavenger hunt! See if you can find the items below related to the mystery. *(Teachers: You have permission to reproduce this form for your students.)*

1. ____ a checkerboard

2. ____ an apron

3. ____ a picture of Buffalo Bill

4. ____ a water balloon

5. ____ a journal

6. ____ a skateboard

7. ____ some cornmeal

8. ____ an egg

9. ____ a cowboy hat

10. ____ a pair of suspenders

TECH CONNECTS

Hey, kids!
Visit www.carolemarshmysteries.com to:

Join the Carole Marsh Mysteries Fan Club!

Write one sensational sentence using all five
SAT words in the glossary!

Download a Prairie Word Search!

Take a Pop Quiz!

Download a Scavenger Hunt!

Learn Pioneer Trivia!

What Kids Say About
Carole Marsh Mysteries . . .

I love the real locations! Reading the book always makes me want to go and visit them all on our next family vacation. My Mom says maybe, but I can't wait!

One day, I want to be a real kid in one of Ms. Marsh's mystery books. I think it would be fun, and I think I am a real character anyway. I filled out the application and sent it in and am keeping my fingers crossed!

History was not my favorite subject until I starting reading Carole Marsh Mysteries. Ms. Marsh really brings history to life. Also, she leaves room for the scary and fun.

I think Christina is so smart and brave. She is lucky to be in the mystery books because she gets to go to a lot of places. I always wonder just how much of the book is true and what is made up. Trying to figure that out is fun!

Grant is cool and funny! He makes me laugh a lot!!

I like that there are boys and girls in the story of different ages. Some mysteries I outgrow, but I can always find a favorite character to identify with in these books.

They are scary, but not too scary. They are funny. I learn a lot. There is always food which makes me hungry. I feel like I am there.

What Parents and Teachers Say About Carole Marsh Mysteries . . .

I think kids love these books because they have such a wealth of detail. I know I learn a lot reading them! It's an engaging way to look at the history of any place or event. I always say I'm only going to read one chapter to the kids, but that never happens—it's always two or three, at least!
—Librarian

Reading the mystery and going on the field trip—Scavenger Hunt in hand—was the most fun our class ever had! It really brought the place and its history to life. They loved the real kids characters and all the humor. I loved seeing them learn that reading is an experience to enjoy! —4th grade teacher

Carole Marsh is really on to something with these unique mysteries. They are so clever; kids want to read them all. The Teacher's Guides are chock full of activities, recipes, and additional fascinating information. My kids thought I was an expert on the subject—and with this tool, I felt like it!
—3rd grade teacher

My students loved writing their own mystery book! Ms. Marsh's reproducible guidelines are a real jewel. They learned about copyright and ended up with their own book they were so proud of!
—Reading/Writing Teacher

"The kids seem very realistic—my children seemed to relate to the characters. Also, it is educational by expanding their knowledge about the famous places in the books."

"They are what children like: mysteries and adventures with children they can relate to."

"Encourages reading for pleasure."

"This series is great. It can be used for reluctant readers, and as a history supplement."